Peppa Pig

Fun at the Fair

Today, Peppa and her family are at the funfair.
"Snort! Slidey, slidey!" giggles George.
"George wants to go on the
helter-skelter," says Daddy Pig.
Daddy Pig and George head off to
the helter-skelter.

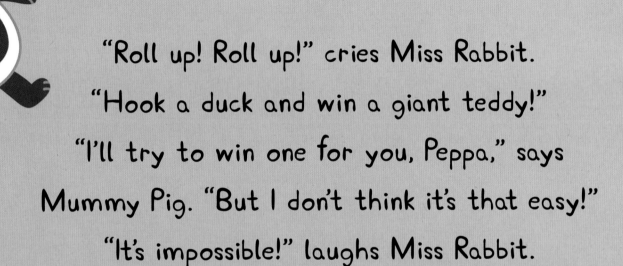

"Roll up! Roll up!" cries Miss Rabbit. "Hook a duck and win a giant teddy!" "I'll try to win one for you, Peppa," says Mummy Pig. "But I don't think it's that easy!" "It's impossible!" laughs Miss Rabbit. "We'll see about that!" cries Mummy Pig.

Sploosh! Mummy Pig has hooked a duck!

"Hooray!" cheers Peppa.

"That's amazing!" cries Miss Rabbit.

"Here's your giant teddy!"

"Wouldn't you like a little teddy instead, Peppa?"

"No way!" giggles Peppa, happily.

George and Daddy Pig are at the helter-skelter.
"Hmm, it's a bit high, George. Are you sure you
want to have a go?" asks Daddy Pig.
George giggles and runs up the stairs to the top.
It's a bit too high and George starts to cry.
"Don't worry, George. I'll come up with you,"
says Daddy Pig.

"Hee, hee! Weeeeeeee!" cries George,
sliding all the way down the helter-skelter.
Now, George is having too much fun to be scared.
"It is a bit high," says Daddy Pig nervously.
Daddy Pig is more scared than George.
Oops! Daddy Pig slips down the slide!

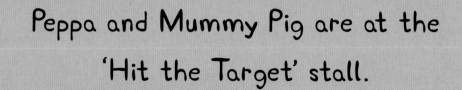

Peppa and Mummy Pig are at the
'Hit the Target' stall.

"You can do that easily, Mummy," says Peppa.

"Ho! Ho! You can try!" Mr Labrador laughs.

Mummy Pig picks up the bow and arrow and aims . . .

Whoosh!
The arrow hits the target
right in the middle.

Mummy Pig wins again!

"Unbelievable," cries Mr Labrador. "Here's your teddy!"

"Hooray!" cheers Peppa.

Now she has two giant teddies.

Daddy Pig and George are
riding on the big wheel. George loves it,
but Daddy Pig is a little bit scared.
"This really is high!" says Daddy Pig, as the
big wheel goes round and round.
"Hee, hee! Snort!" giggles George.

Daddy Pig and George find Peppa and Mummy Pig.
"Hit this button with a hammer," says
Mr Bull. "If the bell rings, you win a prize!"
"I'll have a go," says Daddy Pig. "Stand back!"
"I think you're a bit wobbly from the big wheel!"
says Mummy Pig.

"What?" says Mummy Pig, crossly.
"Give . . . me . . . that . . . hammer!"
Whack! Mummy Pig hits the button
as hard as she can.
The bell rings loudly. Ding! Ding! Ding!

Everyone is very impressed. Mummy Pig wins
all the giant teddies at the fair!

"Hooray!" cheers Peppa and she gives all of
her friends one giant teddy bear each.
"Hooray!" everyone cheers. "We love funfairs!"